To:
Elijah + Tristeen

Love Tasha

REALLY

BAAAAAAAAAAAAAAAAAAAAAD!

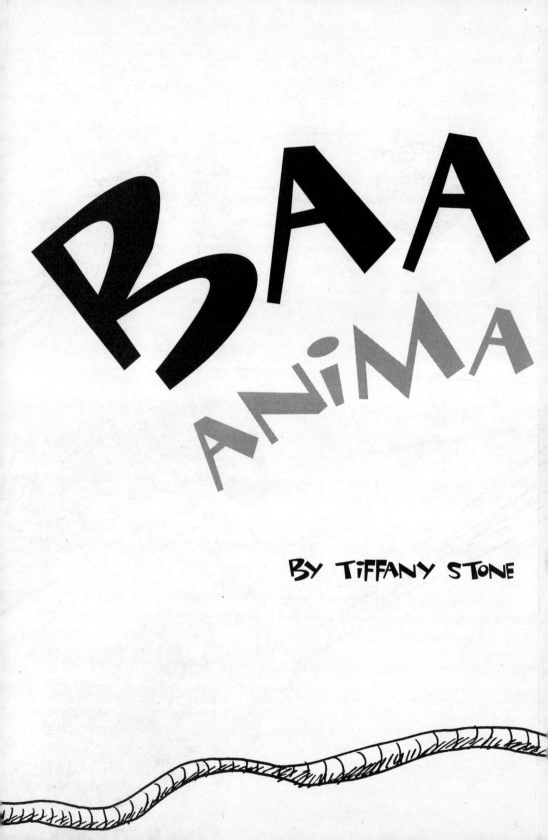

BAA
ANIMA

BY TIFFANY STONE

A A D
L S

ILLUSTRATIONS BY CHRISTINA LEIST

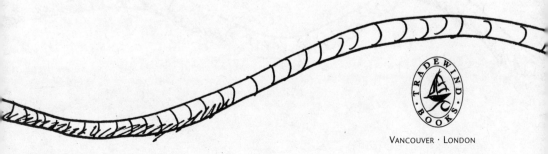

VANCOUVER · LONDON

Published simultaneously in 2006 in Great Britain and Canada by
TRADEWIND BOOKS LIMITED **www.tradewindbooks.com**
Distribution and representation in Canada by Publishers Group Canada
Distribution and representation in the UK by TURNAROUND www.turnaround-uk.com

Book design by Elisa Gutiérrez

LIBRARY AND ARCHIVES CANADA CATALOGUING IN PUBLICATION

Stone, Tiffany, 1967-
    Baad animals / by Tiffany Stone ; illustrated by Christina Leist.

Poems.
ISBN-13: 978-1-896580-36-4
ISBN-10: 1-896580-36-X

    1. Animals--Juvenile poetry. I. Title.

PS8637.T66B22 2006   jC811'.6   C2006-902292-5

CATALOGUING-IN-PUBLICATION DATA for this book available from the British Library.

Printed and bound in Canada   10 9 8 7 6 5 4 3 2 1

Printed on ancient-forest-friendly paper using vegetable-based ink.

The publisher wishes to thank the Government of Canada and Canadian Heritage for their financial support through the Canada Council for the Arts, the Book Publishing Industry Development Program (BPIDP) and the Association for the Export of Canadian Books. The publisher also wishes to thank the Government of British Columbia for the financial support it has extended through the book publishing tax credit program and the British Columbia Arts Council.

Canada Council **Conseil des Arts**
for the Arts **du Canada**

BRITISH
COLUMBIA
ARTS COUNCIL

In memory of my mum, Janet Stone—love you, miss you and thanks for all the stamps! And for Joan Ford and Gail Roberts, for being such GOOOOOOOOOOOOOOOOOOD adoptive grandmas to Emory, Jewell and Kaslo— T S

Dedicated to those two special individuals who have always wanted me to do what I wanted to do. Thanks to all the head-standing, house-sharing, milchzahn-losing, coffee-shop-chilling, scarf-knitting, adventure-living, always-date-cancelling, mind-opening and in-fairies-gnomes-and-me-believing individuals I met in Vancouver. Thanks for being good friends, uncommon teachers and great inspirations.— C L

WHAT'S HAPPENIN' HERE?

BAAD ANiMALS

Bandits, burglars, cheats.
Kleptomaniacs, robbers, thieves.

We're baad animals.
We're baad animals.

Our language is coarse. Our wool is, too.
We dye it green and pink and blue.

We're baad animals.
We're baad animals.

If you can't sleep, don't count us sheep.
We'll give you nightmares, make you weep.

We're baad animals.
We're baad animals.

If we meet you after dark
wearing a sweater in the park,
one, two, three...ATTACK!
We'll pounce on you and steal it back.

We're baad animals.
We're baad animals.
Baa baa BAAAAAAAAAAAAAAAAAAAAAD!

THE SECRET LiFE OF SLUGS

Slugs seem sluggish.
Slugs seem slow.
But slugs have a secret
you don't know.
Slugs are sneaky.
Slugs pretend.
When no one's looking,
their feet descend.
And under cover of the dark,
slugs run races in the park.

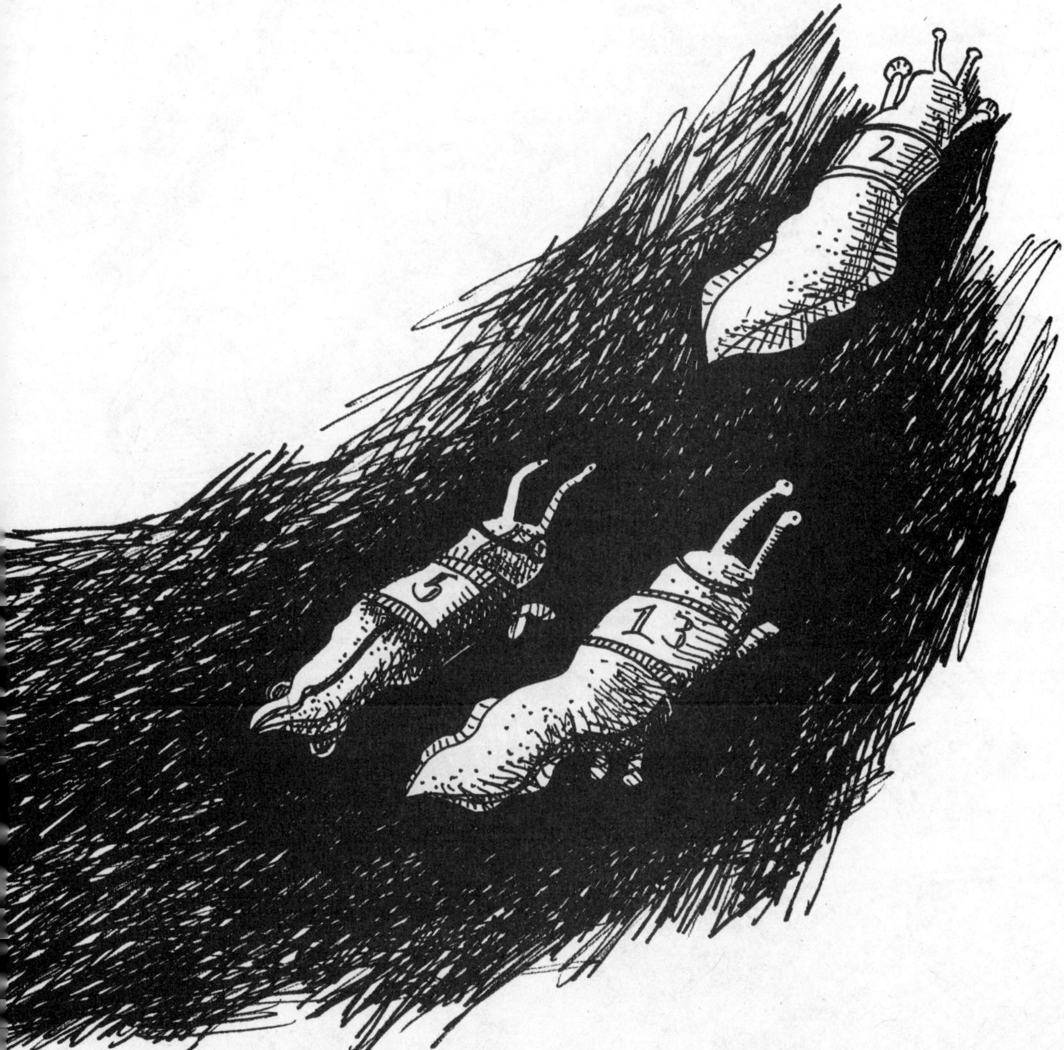
2
5
13

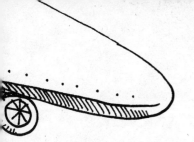

DON'T GIVE A MAGNET TO AN ELEPHANT

Don't give a magnet to an elephant.
He won't handle it with care.
He'll hold it high up in the sky
and pull planes out of the air.
He'll get it stuck to delivery trucks
and bicycles and trains.
He'll cause trouble at construction sites
by sticking to the cranes.
He'll magnetize the city—
every car, bus, van and truck.
Then he'll sneak home to the jungle
and leave everybody stuck.

TYRANNOSAURUS WRECKS

My friends won't visit anymore
not even Nick who lives next door
because of my new dinosaur.
I got him free; he has defects.
He's not cool like everyone expects.
He's a clumsy tyrannosaur that wrecks.
Crunch! There goes my best toy car!
Squish! Mum's jumbo chocolate bar!
Twang! Oh no, Dad, your guitar!
Stumble, bumble, trip, tromp, tread!
Everybody duck your head!
Maybe I'll trade for a stegosaurus
instead....

MENACING MARK

I knew a shark
called Menacing Mark
who never brushed his teeth.
Not even after snacking on
some divers on the reef.
"Cavities, they don't scare me!"
he told me face to face.
"If ten teeth rot, I've got
a hundred more to take their place."
But fearsome Mark forgot one thing—
his awful, stinky breath.
It frightened all his prey away
and soon he starved to death.

ΛΛΛΛΛH!

Look at the baby,
isn't it cute!
What extra-long razor-sharp claws.

Look at the baby,
isn't it sweet!
Is that a full set of teeth in its jaws?

Look at the baby,
so tiny and new,
with spines all over its back.

Look at the baby,
but don't get too close.
It will gobble you up for a snack!

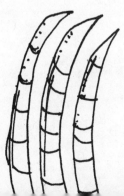

OUR CLUB

We're starting a club,
a club to complain,
for all us poor victims
of strange-sounding names.
We welcome you, aye-aye.
Hello, kinkajou.
And bongo and numbat
and you, wallaroo.
Skink, won't you join us
and bring manatee,
zebu, echidna?
Invite okapi.
Let's call capybara,
then meet without fail
to find those who named us
and THROW THEM IN JAIL!

STRIPES

Stripes on Monday,
Tuesday, Wednesday.
Stripes the whole week through.

Stripes in spring
and summer, autumn.
Stripes in winter, too.
Stripes are for
old BORING zebras,
like my mum and dad.
Not for me—
a little paint
and now I'm dressed in plaid.

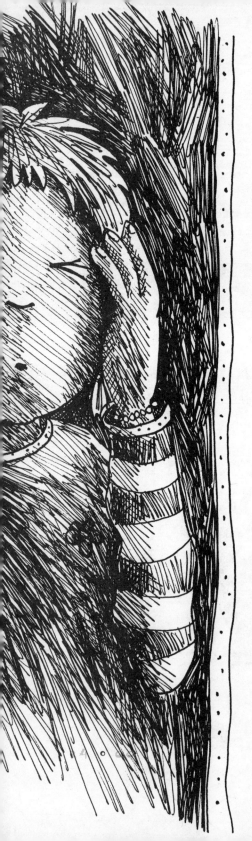

SCARY POEM

You think that noise
you hear at night
the one that gives you
such a fright
is something M A S S I V E
moving 'round
talons tapping
on the ground.
Your parents say
it's nothing but
you squeeze your eyelids
tighter shut
and yet you cannot
sleep at all
with all that tapping
in the hall.
It's getting closer
faster, too.
Hee-hee ha-ha
the joke's on you.
There is no monster
no indeed.
Just me
a dancing millipede!

SHOCKING!

A burp from a buffalo,
a toot from a moose—
impolite.
But *I'm* the rudest!
I'm a grizzly bear
with no fur *anywhere*.
The world's first forest nudist.

26 0 27

MR WOLF

I'm not bad,
I'm just no good
at acting like
you think I should.
No huff 'n' puff
for piggy snacks.
I'd surely have
a heart attack.
No dressing up
in Granny's clothes.
I'm much too fat
to fit in those.
My fangs are loose,
my muscles weak.
I'm going bald,
my joints all creak.
I need a nap
before it's noon.
Sigh....
This wolf must retire soon!

CREATURE

I've got fifty-five feet,
no neck and no nose
but nine nostrils
as big as your fist.

I sting and explode
and ooze purple pus.
And your mum says
that I don't exist!

LYIN'

I promise not to eat you,
raw or roasted on a fire.

BURP!

You shouldn't have believed me.
Every lion is a liar.

RULES

Do not tie knots
in unsuspecting snakes.
Do not hop on hippos' heads
to get across the lake.
Do not cheat when playing chess
with cheetahs late at night.
It may not be illegal
but that doesn't make it right.
Do not connect a leopard's spots
or toot a rhino's horn.
Laugh at a hyena
and you'll wish that you weren't born.
Do not subtract with adders.
Do not pinch a chimpanzee.
Do not, do not, do not, do NOT
times ninety-nine
times three!

iF YOU KNEW
WHAT THE GNU KNEW

If you knew what the gnu knew,
you'd be ultra super wise.
You'd be smarter than the scientists
and all the brainy guys.
The gnu knows all the new news
but you'll never be as bright
cuz she keeps all that gnu knowledge
in her noggin locked up tight.

WHEN PIGS MAKE PANCAKES

When pigs make pancakes,
batter flies
all over the barnyard
out of the sties.

When pigs flip them,
those pancakes stick
to every cow, every horse,
every lamb, every chick.

And when pigs pour syrup,
it's more than a drop.
They slosh it all over
as if it were slop.

Pigs don't even *like* pancakes,
at least not to eat.
Making a mess
is the true piggy treat.

i'M TiRED oF BEiNG A TEDDY

I'm tired of being a teddy.
I'm tired of being so sweet.
I'm tired of being cuddled
and carried around by my feet.

I'm tired of babies and children.
I'm tired of Mummy and Dad.
I'm tired of being good.
But I'm too lazy to learn to be bad.

A YOUNG SEAHORSE'S COMPLAINT

Daddy's belly's getting big.
It's so unfair. Boo hoo!
He's going to have more babies soon.
Disgusting! Gross! P-ew!
I have seven hundred sisters
and a thousand brothers, too.
The waterbed is crowded.
Our bathroom has a queue.
My mum never remembers—
my name is *Sarah*, not Sue.

I DON'T NEED A SINGLE SIBLING MORE!
But what am I to do?
Oh, I wish I was an ONLY CHILD
with my very own tank in the zoo.

TUNA FISH RAP

No bath for me,
I live in the sea.
I'm never dry;
I'm always clean.
I'm the cleanest creature
you've ever seen.
But if I could have
one magic wish,
I'd wish I wasn't
a clean old fish.
I'd wish for a bucket
full of dirt and crud.
Then I'd dump it in the ocean
and I'd make some mud—
grubby mud,
messy mud,
yucky, mucky mud.

MY CAT GOT iNTO THE PEANUT BUTTER

My cat got into the peanut butter.
My cat got into the jelly.
She smeared some on her whiskers
and she rubbed some on her belly.
She dipped her tail in like a brush
and painted on the wall.
She left pawprints on the counter.
She left pawprints in the hall.
She didn't make a sandwich
but she made a sticky mess.
I shouldn't have taught her
how to open jars, I guess.

GIRAFFES LIVE IN THE CITY

Giraffes live in the city
but they wear clever disguises
to make you think they're construction cranes
of many different sizes.
But at night when no one's looking,
they're giraffes again, not cranes
and they like to saunter single file
down alleyways and lanes.
They are searching for their suppers
'midst the skyscrapers and the shops
and when they find the tallest buildings,
they nibble off the tops.
Then early in the morning,
they are back to being cranes.
They repair the damage they caused at night
before anyone complains.

CHOCOLATE MOOSE

Chocolate Moose was on the loose,
searching for dessert.
He foraged in the forest
but all he found was dirt.
He marched through many marshes,
crossed a river and a stream—
looking for a treat to eat,
some cookies or ice cream.
A pie, a pudding or perhaps
some pralines he could chew.
But he had no luck. No, none at all.
That is, till he met YOU!
You were eating candy in your tent.
Every inch of you was sticky.
From behind a tree leaped Chocolate Moose
and gave you a GREAT BIG lick.
He licked and licked

and licked and licked and licked and licked and licked and licked and licked and licked and licked and licked and licked and licked and licked and licked and licked.

i SCREAM

No cheese, no yogurt,
no cream, no butter.
Get away with that bucket.
Keep it far from my udder.
We bovines are not
as calm as we seem.
Just try to milk me,
you'll hear this cow
SCREAM!!!!!!!!!!!!!!

YUM!

I'm making a DEE-licious stew—
with eggshells and dryer lint, too.
Mouldy peel from an orange
and ten-day-old porridge—
too tasty to share it with YOU!

I'm making a YUM-scrummy treat.
It's flavour can never be beat.
Breakfast, dinner, dessert,
more luscious than dirt—
but YOU can't have any to eat!

I'm making a WORM-famous feast—
the best in the west and the east.
And the north and the south.
Go away. Close your mouth.
You're not getting EVEN ONE PIECE!

A SLOTH WENT ON VACATION

A sloth went on vacation
but he didn't get too far
cuz it took him eighteen hours
just to climb into his car.

NOT THE PORCUPINE

There are too many animals asleep in my bed.
ONE OF THEM HAS GOT TO GO!
Should it be the porcupine with her prickly quills?
Not the porcupine. No.
How about the tiger with his teeth and claws?
Not the tiger either. No.
The cobra?
The skunk?
The humungous blue whale?
No. All of those can stay.
But that tiny shrew who snores so loud,
SEND HER FAR AWAY!

52 O 53

BLACK AND WHITE BLUES

A skunk's supposed
to be black and white
but I'm blue
but I'm blue
but I'm blue
day and night.

I'm a skunk
who's sunk
in a deep,
deep
funk
cuz my stink
cuz my stink
cuz my stink's
come unstunk.

O-o-dour's weak, not strong.
Ste-e-ench is bye-bye, gone.

Woe is me!
Woe is me!
Woe is me-e-e-eeeeeee!

(Better hide in a pile of dirty laundry.)

iF YOU'RE THiNKiNG OF GiViNG A TORTOiSE A TiCKLE

If you're thinking of giving
a tortoise a tickle,
I warn you you'd better think twice.
Cuz a tortoise who's tickled
is quick to reveal that
she's not necessarily nice.

She's deceptively docile
and older than old but
just sneak up and tickle her shell.
Goodness gracious, she'll knock you
right out of your socks and
then tickle your feet till you yell.

DEAR ANTIES

You're invited
to a party in the park.
Bring your uncles. Bring your cousins.
Cuz it's sure to be a lark.
Bring your grannies. Bring your grandpas.
Better hurry. Don't be late!
Even bring your bitty babies.
They can carry twice their weight.
Bring your in-laws. Bring your outlaws.
Bring your knives and forks and spoons.
Meet us where the people picnic.

Signed,

tHE CROWS aND tHE RaCCOONS

UNCRABBY

I'm not crabby in the morning.
Not in the afternoon.
I'm not crabby in November.
Not crabby when it's June.
I'm not crabby when my day has been
EXTRAORDINARILY BAD!
Not even when my brother's mean.
Or when my mum is mad!
I'm never EVER crabby.
I simply refuse to be.
I'm a rebellious crustacean—
the uncrabbiest crab in the sea.

GiMME

Gimme a straw,
I need a cold drink.
But not from a cup
or a bowl or the sink.
From the toilet, of course.
Well, what did ya think?
I'm a dog, I got class.
I sip, so polite.
So gimme a straw.
Yeah, you heard me, that's right.

GOODNIGHT

Goodnight and be careful
of humans with swatters.
They'll squish your mum's sons
and they'll squash your dad's daughters.

They'll spritz you with sprays
that'll make you drop dead
and kill all your cousins
and dear Uncle Fred.
Life is tough for us bugs
who come out late at night
for a quick drink of blood
or a much bigger bite.
So far I've been lucky
but you can't count on that.
So goodnight and be careful,
my insect friends—

SPLAT!